little HALLOWEEN

Ana,
Trick or treat?
Xo. Eva Marks

EVA MARKS

Copyright © 2022 by Eva Marks

All rights reserved.

No portion of this book may be reproduced in any form without written permission from the author, except as permitted by U.S. copyright law.

This is a work of fiction. Any names, characters, places or incidents are products of the author's imagination and used in fictious manner. Any resemblance to actual people, places or events is purely coincidental or fictionalized.

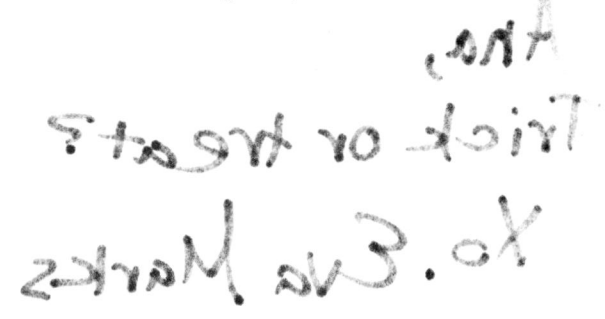

Ana,

Trick or treat?

Xo. Eva Marks

A Note from the Author

Little Halloween is a steamy novella, containing explicit and graphic scenes and kinks intended for mature audiences only.

Trigger Warnings

Bondage, edging, some toys, a touch of degradation, sex club, pet play and exhibitionism.

About the Book

This Halloween he has a special treat and trick for her…

After overcoming our differences, I'm finally engaged to Hudson, my old boss and millionaire CFO.

We're madly in love and I can't complain when he constantly cherishes, coddles me and calls me his good girl.

I can't and won't, even if I miss his harsh domineering side at times.

But my older fiancé, who reads me like a book, can tell I have doubts, and he knows just how to put them to rest.

This Halloween, at an adult club party, Hudson will show me and everyone around once and for all exactly what my Sir is made of.

CHAPTER ONE
Avery

"Little blue." Hudson's strict voice is a harsh caress, the dull spine of a sharp knife.

It's his calling, the demand for me to recenter.

Always used at the right place and right time.

Because my fiancé is the master of the delicate art of keeping me in line.

It usually puts an end to my worries so I can't be blamed for how I'm almost angered at the fact that it doesn't happen now. I banked on it having the same effect on me today.

It doesn't.

All thanks to my stupid, weak mind.

"Hudson, I can't do this." My words are spoken with defiance, a tone I've never dared to address him with four months ago.

It's not because he instills fear in me. Hudson isn't remotely close to being a violent man. Nothing like that. The reason I hadn't defied him until recently—and not for the three years we were strictly co-workers—was my own need to please him had trumped everything else.

Then where is it now? And who am I without it?

I stare at my image in the mirror at Hudson's place—now our home, at the long sapphire-blue gown Hudson chose for me. The soft chiffon strapless dress fits my curves perfectly, the hem reaching just above the floor when I'm in my heels.

Its sweetheart neckline exposes the exact amount of cleavage, nothing too vulgar, just enough for the tops of my breasts to show. It also reveals the leather collar with black lace he ceremoniously put around my neck two months ago.

Akin to the classy cleavage, there's nothing about the ownership collar, either. Especially since we don't want to upset our surroundings, or in this case, the guests at my fiancé's corporate Halloween party and my old workplace.

Whitlock.

AKA the source of my heightened awareness with sprinkles of defiance on top.

At the beginning of Hudson's and my relationship, Albert Benjamin, the COO of Whitlock, caught us having lunch together. He connected the dots—not to mention mocked me in the process—and spread the news about us.

People love gossip. They love a juicy age-gap, workplace forbidden romance.

So when he told them about the twenty-four-year-old *ex*-marketing associate who spent countless hours in meetings with the thirty-seven-year-old divorced CFO, they ate it right up.

When he suggested our meetings should've been held between Hudson and the marketing director, not me, they inhaled it like they'd die without it. *Special* meetings they called it behind Hudson's back. How else could my fiancé and I explain our engagement less than a year after quitting my job at Whitlock?

Let the record show, we didn't do anything during the years I worked there, other than pine for each other. Hudson is a professional down to the bone. A respectful man who had my reputation at the forefront of his mind, even when it hurt him to stay away.

But try telling them that.

Vultures.

Hudson wouldn't admit to me they were talking about us, hadn't so much as hinted anything was wrong. Behind his all-encompassing, strong, and cold exterior hides a sweet, caring, and thoughtful man who'd do everything in his power to keep me out of harm's way.

Unless, of course, at least one of us is fully naked in bed, our kitchen, or in our secret, newly-renovated room.

Which is totally beside the point.

The point is—I know.

My old teammate, Rina, made sure to text me the 411 on all things Hudson and Avery out of spite for me. Since I quit the company, Hudson hasn't treated her with care and attentiveness as he had me, hasn't spent hours explaining to her the roots of the business. Half the time, he calls her boss for meetings he would've normally held with me.

She tells me that too, and I honestly can't blame her for being bitter. I feel for Rina, my soft side allowing her to spam me with messages, to pretend it doesn't bother me that people judge us. But maybe, just maybe, it does.

"What did you say?"

My fiancé appears behind me. His tall, broad frame in my favorite black suit is the dark shadow I never want to go without. His sharp green eyes penetrate me through our reflection, his dark-blond hair is so immaculately styled I want to run my hands through it.

If only tonight would stop bothering me this badly.

"I said—" I start, my tone a tad exasperated with the situation, and maybe a little of myself.

Truth is, having people gossip is only a part of why I talk back to him.

The other two parts are all on me.

I have unrealistic expectations of our relationship, hoping it won't change. It's dumb, I'm aware of it. I can't expect us to sneak around, mainly because *I* told Hudson I don't want us to be a secret. In hindsight, I wish I'd stretched that period. I recognized too late how it made me something more than a girlfriend, but the woman he couldn't stop himself from wanting, the one he broke his rules for. His sexy secret.

Then there's my irrational disappointment with Hudson's internal give and take. Hudson's kind and nourishing side blends slowly into the rough one I've known for years. He does it elegantly, caring and loving me without neglecting to be rough when he fucks me. Everyone should aspire to have that in a spouse, so why not me?

I'm not saying that I love him any less than I did yesterday, or that I'd in any shape or form stop loving him tomorrow. Miles from that.

For this little girl, Hudson will forever be the first ray of sun after a long night, the deliverer of pain and the conduit of pleasure. My controlling, domineering, sinfully sexy, and hot as shit fiancé.

My Sir.

That's why I hate feeling this way. I hate bitching instead of appreciating him. I just can't control this sick need to rile him up, to have him this possessive of me again outside of the bedroom and more than the few Dom and sub habits we added to our relationship.

Maybe even make him crazy enough at the party to drag me to the bathroom and bring me to my knees to suck him off.

A girl can dream.

Five fingers wrap around my long brown hair.

Sometimes, that girl's dreams come true.

"The mouth on you." He tugs at my hair, drawing my ear to his lips. His mouth smells of peppermint, his body of his cologne I'm crazy for. "I think you're confused, little. Wouldn't you say?"

"Hudson—" I sigh. I'm being whiny on purpose. He's right. I'm not myself today. I need my fix, need him to put me back together again like only he can.

There's another tug at my hair, stronger this time, accompanied by a bite to my neck. "Is that how you address me?"

"I—"

His large palm connects with my ass, creating a loud slap echoing in the room.

My teeth sink to the inside of my cheek, though it doesn't take away from the sting on my flesh. It stays there, changing and morphing to a sweet delight that reaches my clit.

It's exactly what I wanted, and I squirm under his touch, squeezing my thighs and rubbing the wetness soaking my thong.

"Wrong. Answer." He spanks the same spot twice, one for each word.

His breath is at my neck now, his voice threatening. "Try again."

I lower my eyes to find his blazing green ones glowering at me through the mirror. "Sir, I—"

Hudson massages the sensitive area where he spanked me, a smirk forming on the strong lines of his lips. "Better. Continue."

"Sir, I can't—"

Slap.

"What did I say about your can'ts?"

"You said the only can't is in *there's nothing I can't do*."

His palm leaves my ass, trailing up my body in a possessive hold, eventually reaching my collar. "That's true."

Hudson's index finger toys with the center ring, pulling it forward and down. My neck and the roots of my hair stretch as I'm pulled in two opposite directions, yet I say nothing.

In my silence, I accept his tough, grounding love. I revel in it. Endorphins stream seamlessly to my veins, clearing my head. No more useless thoughts about gossiping idiots or turning back the clock.

When he handles me like that, I'm helpless against resisting, against anger. I'm above petty feelings, trusting Hudson will always make them right. I stand grounded, and at the same time, I float.

"Why are you wearing this collar, little blue?" He pins his long, hard cock to my ass. "Why do you think it was crucial for me to put it on you? Why was it more important and had to be done earlier than our wedding ceremony?"

My throat is clogged, bits of emotion blocking air in and out. This collar, much like Hudson, means everything to me.

"To show me you love me."

"Good girl." His mouth sucks on my shoulder. The immediate arousal fries my brain and melts my insides. "There's more to it, though."

My nipples are hard, my clit has a pulse of its own, and my lips are so parched my tongue slips out to lick them.

Hudson hones in on the gesture, humming in approval. "Talk to me."

"So I have a constant reminder that I'm yours. And that together, there's nothing I can't do."

"Correct." His hand leaves my collar, disappearing behind me.

"I'm aware of it." Hudson's knuckles skim the bare skin of my back, lowering along the curve of my spine to land at my dress's zipper. "Thing is, I'm not convinced *you* are."

The sound of the zipper rolling down my body is amplified times a million in the quiet room. Hudson's knuckles scrape the skin as he goes until he reaches the end. The dress flutters and flails to the floor, landing in a blue mess at my feet.

I'm exposed, my blue bra and see-through lace thong doing nothing to hide my body. Sure, I have my thin, satin blue sandals laced on my feet but…that's it.

Hudson casts his eyes to the length of my reflection, oozing boredom. The bulge pressing to my ass says otherwise.

"Into the mirror room." He releases me, his eyebrow rising in a challenge. "Do not make me wait."

CHAPTER TWO
Hudson

I'm not easily bothered. Money and status fix nearly everything, and I have both. Clean house, tailor-made outfits, a table in every restaurant in town, comprehensive health insurance—they're at an arm's reach. All I need to do to get them is make a phone call and poof, it's there.

The one thing I want the most, though, is not money or what my position as a CFO can buy me. Having Avery feel like the confident queen she is every hour of the day is something I have to work for, and I do.

I want her to remember twenty-four seven, even in her sleep, that there's nothing she can't do, that nothing and no one is standing in her way to be whomever it is she wants to be. I'll be damned if I'll allow shallow office gossip to force my hand into hiding her. It's never gonna happen. Never.

So I asked her to be my date for this dance, to give them all a big fuck you, Kent family style. But this is a learning opportunity for her, and I'm leveraging it to her advantage by sending her to the mirror room.

Being late doesn't bother me. Seeing Avery doubt herself, that's a huge spot on my radar I'm all too eager to wipe away.

I watch her walk on her heels. Her round, mildly red butt sways and bounces as she treads on them across the hallway. I bide my time, staying put, not rushing to follow my soon-to-be-wife.

The wall I pull up between us is for her benefit, to pick up where her confidence failed her. As my sub, she's grounded, shielded, and navigates safely to her happy place when I remind her who she belongs to.

Not stalking after her is a challenge, but the advantages outweigh the selfishness of wanting to hug her.

Most days, anyway. On others, when I was hard for her at the office and I missed her too much, I skip any ceremony and charge at her.

Fortunately, today, we're saved from my impatience.

Avery opens the door we keep locked from the outside world. My gait is slow and calculated behind her, making it past the doorway and into the dark room.

The light from the hallway gives me a view of Avery. The dim light highlights the tenderness of her body, her soft lips, the shine of her silky hair. She sits in the center like the good girl she is, practiced and cognizant of how I expect to find her.

During the months we've been together, we've educated ourselves on BDSM and the power exchange lifestyle. We did it to pour more meaning into our love language, to enhance our connection, to understand the meaning behind our intrinsic desires.

We're not defined by them, though. Living these habits is an add-on, a natural extension of how both of us perceived our relationship. We take some; others, we pass on.

And this one, of her waiting for me, is definitely one we keep.

Avery's sandals and thong are placed to the side, and she sits on her heels, spreading her knees and baring her wet cunt to me. Her palms face upward while her blue eyes are downcast, waiting for my instructions.

Metaphorically speaking, I could look at her in this position for hours. I would never tire from having her as my partner and my submissive. Avery isn't just the pot to my kettle; she was created from my very own rib.

The harsh lights I switch on paint the room white. They're not my favorite, but then again, they're not for me.

I'm not the one who has to witness what a fucking wonder they are on any of the mirrors we installed across the room.

She is.

I'm laser-beam focused on where my mind always is. On my little one. My cock is hard and heavy in my suit pants, my heart thrumming at a steady pace. I have to be in control of my physical reactions to her for our relationship to work.

I can't get off on possessing her if I lack that quality in myself.

"I'm so pleased with you." I stand in front of her, patting her head.

My groin and her face are inches apart, yet she keeps looking down. She won't move unless I say otherwise.

"Look at me."

She gazes up at me, batting her long eyelashes and pouting her lips the way she knows makes my blood boil.

It's on the tip of my tongue to tell her I love her.

"Stand up." I flick my fingers to the ceiling to accompany my command.

She rises elegantly to her adorable five-foot-three inches, focusing on me even as I shift my attention elsewhere.

"You've been acting out, Blue." I pull on the handcuffs attached to the rope hung on hooks in the ceiling.

Here, in this room, she knows better than to argue or give me attitude.

Her eyes linger on me while I undo the leather belt buckles. I don't spare her a glance; don't pay attention to her attentive stare. Pity won't do her any good.

"Hands in the air," I instruct her once the cuffs are unbuckled.

She does.

I still don't look her in the eye while working on the cuffs. I secure them to her wrists, tight enough to restrain her without causing damage. She loves the pain that accompanies the pressure. I don't have to look at her to know her nipples are hard. I don't have to slip a finger into her cunt for proof she's soaked.

But I don't care for any of that now. My goal, through this pain, is to keep her aware.

I spin her to the face away from me. In her reflection, I see her lips part in surprise, then clamp shut.

"That's right, you do not talk unless spoken to." I slip a hand to her front, tapping on what I'm sure is her aching clit as a reward.

Her face is expressionless, her throat bobs in her attempt to suppress a moan.

"You've been very good in this room." My arm gestures to the room around us, then back to shoving two fingers in her pussy. "And here." My fingers dip deeper into her. "Cunt sopping, tits ready for me. Very, very good, little one."

"Thank you," she sighs.

I forgive her for speaking. Showing her gratitude and being eager to please me are two characteristics that have been imprinted on her from the moment we met. I would never admonish her for wanting to please me.

For other things, however… "In here, though?"—I tap her temple—"this needs some fixing. Do you understand me?"

"Yes, Sir."

I remove my hand from her pussy, sucking in one wet finger. The second one, I push inside her mouth. She sucks it dry, doing what's expected of her.

"Very good." Taking a handkerchief out of an inner pocket of my suit jacket, I dry them off. "About your lesson. There are a few ways we can go about it."

My hands snake under her armpit, my arms caging in her breasts. I cup her jaw, directing her face to the mirror so she can't escape our reflection.

"I'm going to ask you a few questions. You tell me the truth, and I'll fuck you however you like. I see you lying to me—and be sure that I will—there'll be consequences. Understood?"

Her impulses instruct her to nod, but I firm my grip on Avery's jaw. A demonstration of how I hold the control on those as well.

"Words."

"Yes, Sir."

"Let's start, then." I suck in a breath, inhaling the scent of her shampoo, of her clean body mist, and ignore it. "Why do you care what people at Whitlock think?"

"I don'—"

Slap. I hit her right breast, pinching the nipple tight and tugging it forward.

"Try again."

"It's nothing. I don't care." She moans, reaching the part where the pain morphs into pleasure.

I let go of her nipple and walk to the closet where we keep our sex toys. From the top shelf, I pull out the black leather flogger and return to my hanging, brat of a fiancée.

The red spot on her ass gets the first smack, and the red darkens some more. "I don't like what I'm hearing, little."

"Hud—"

Another two smacks on her bruised cheek, a third on the other.

"Sir, please."

Tears murk her voice. I look up to see her head bowed down and her long, brown locks hanging on either side of her.

Having her reach a breaking point worries me. "Are you okay, Avery?"

"Yes."

"Do you need to use your safeword?" I rub her behind carefully. "I'll stop whenever you need me to."

"No, Sir." She inhales a long breath. "I'm okay.".

"You ready to tell me why we have a problem?"

"It's nothing. Really."

"All right, Avery." She glances up, thinking we're done. Not by a mile.

"Nothing is a seven-letter word." I run the flogger up and down her back, lowering it to linger on her thighs. "You seem to like it so much, so you'll get seven strokes. And you will count each of them."

We glare at each other through the mirror. Her eyes darken. There's no denying her arousal. There's definitely no hiding mine.

"Thank you, Sir."

"Thank me later." I move back, holding my arm up. "Count."

And she does.

"One, two, three," she grunts fast, matching the pace I spank her butt cheek.

"Four." Comes next on her right, red one. "Five, Six." I spread her thighs, showing no mercy there either.

"Seven," she growls when I finish my punishment on her right, sweltering butt cheek.

My breaths are labored, a result of exertion as well as arousal. I lock my emotions out of sight, instilling indifference into my gaze on my way to Avery's front.

We stare at each other. She earned the timeout, the relief. It's the place her brain can regroup and provide me with the truth. For a few seconds, I caress her neck with one palm, swiping the hairs of the flogger on her cunt.

She's wonderful, my little with her crimson red cheeks. "Talk to me. What's going on?"

"People."

"Fuck people." I spit out, my mouth working faster than my brain. I rush to correct myself, to calm down. "Come on, tell me more."

"They gossip." Her tongue swipes at her bottom lip. "They think I'm a slut. That I opened my legs to get special attention."

"Blue." Holding two fingers beneath her chin, I lift her face to me. "Fuck. People."

"Albert…"

The distance is killing me. I can't fucking take it anymore.

I pull her head toward me, pressing our mouths together in a kiss, coaxing her lips open. My tongue drags along her teeth, swirling with hers. I tell her in so many words that no one else matters.

It's not enough to relieve the nagging feeling in my chest.

"I still go back to that day, that lunch Albert treated you like…" The drumbeat in my head nearly deafens me with rage that I shove down. "That fucker. I was wrong not to jump at him and fuck the consequences. I swear, that day never left me, and—"

"Really?" She breaks character, and I can't be mad at it just as I can't reproach her thank yous.

I can't, because it was me who fucked up. Because he mocked her for having daddy issues—which, even if she had them, so fucking what—and I worried about getting arrested for punching his smug little smile in.

"Yes, really." I return to character, my tone stern and my posture erect. "You don't have to worry about that anymore. Anyone who mistreats you today will have hell to pay. I take care of what's mine. I won't falter a second time."

"You'll do it? For me?" Avery's eyes gloss over, a new wave of unshed tears brimming.

For a lack of a better explanation, I chalk it off to the emotional strain of being hung for the last minute or two, along with the flogging and failing to satisfy me until she decided to talk.

"Yeah, Blue. I will."

The flogger is no longer necessary, and I dump it to the side. I take a step forward, releasing the rope that holds Avery in place while my arm is wrapped around her midriff to secure her.

"You trust me?" The question is directed to her current state, but also to my promise of never failing her again.

"I do." Her lips are an inch from mine, though I won't touch them.

Let me rephrase. My *lips* won't touch them.

Because they're going to be filled with my cock.

"Good, since in the next few minutes, you'll have nothing but trust to grasp onto."

CHAPTER THREE
Avery

God, I love this man.

Hudson's promise to come to my defense serves as a balm to my anxiety. It satisfies me instantly, filling me to the brim with an overflowing need to thank him, to love him, to be his good girl.

I'm dripping with the need to do anything in my power to satisfy him. On my knees, hung from the ceiling, I'll find a way. Fuck my burning thighs and shaking biceps.

Nothing in this world matters but satisfying Sir. I will obey him however he sees fit, I'll cry and spit and let him use my cunt and mouth whichever way he likes. I'll do it all to please him, will not stop until I hear his praise. Anything and everything.

"Let me be clear." He tugs at his black belt as he stands above me, opening the buckle. His fly is next, revealing the outline of his thick cock, the drop of precum, his want for me.

"No one's opinion, and I mean no one's"—his boxers come off and I'm salivating at the mouth—"is as important as mine."

I eye him from my place on the floor. His dark-blond hair is disheveled in an organized way, his short stubble frames his pinched shut mouth. He's tall, handsome, and menacing. He's mine.

"Yes, Sir." His name is a rasp on my lips. "No one's but yours."

"Good girl."

His expensive shoes tap the wooden floor twice when he closes the distance between us. A second later, Hudson pulls out his cock, placing it on my lips. I could write sonnets about this man's dick, its silky texture, its clean taste, and how it throbs in my presence.

I would suck on it all day if I could.

He holds it upright, brushing the crown along my lips. Another drop of precum dampens my lips, and though I'm dying to taste it, I don't.

Hudson is my Sir, my king. In this room more than anywhere else. I'm aware of my slipup today, that I shouldn't have taken it out on him. And I'm working hard to make up for it.

Hudson's lips quirk in a knowing smirk that doesn't last. He cups my head from behind, his head tilting, his somber voice demanding me, "Open up."

No other word is said when he shoves his entire length into my mouth. His fingers clench on my skull, rumpling my hair while he pulls me back and forth, fucking my mouth for his pleasure.

It's an out-of-body experience, to be so completely owned and safe and guarded by the man you love more than your own self. I relax my throat to let him in farther, and he rewards me.

"You're so good, Avery, my good little girl."

He stops every ten counts to let me breathe, a routine we've mastered over the past few months. Hudson sticks to them so that even when I'm out of air, I always know when my relief is coming. Then he fucks my face again.

I'm panting, moaning onto his dick, which only makes him grip my hair tighter and pound harder into me. In these seconds, while my mouth is being ravaged and I'm staring up at Hudson's clenched jaw, I know another thing. That I'm doing well.

The sensations are overwhelming. My heart pounds vigorously, my breasts heavy and swollen with lust. Between my thighs I'm molten, burning, and with the slightest encouragement, I will undoubtedly come.

And coming without his permission would be the greatest disappointment of them all. Hudson owns my orgasms, and as desperate as I am, I need his approval to have one. I close my lips and suck hard, our safe-signal—for a lack of a better word—for when I'm unable to speak or move.

He removes his cock abruptly, kneeling before me to gauge my expression. With the pad of his thumb, he clears the spit off my jaw, while his eyes search mine for any sign of distress. "Everything okay?"

"I was about to come."

He huffs, biting his lip and shaking his head. "You make me so proud, Avery. Showing me you learned there's only me to please and care for in this world."

"Thank you."

Hudson straightens. One of his hands grips the back of my head again to hold me in place while he loosens the rope to its maximum length. My body goes limp and would've dropped completely to the floor, if not for Hudson's hold.

He thinks of everything, always does. He sees me and he loves me, and I can't, not even if I was being held at a gunpoint, remember why I thought our relationship was anything less than perfect.

"You gave me what I asked for." He lays me down gently to the floor, fixing my hands above my head, still cuffed. His ministrations are tender, his voice is not. "And good behavior is rewarded."

I stay dutifully silent. He stands to discard his shoes, pants, and boxers, revealing his lean pair of legs and his glistening cock.

I want—no, I need—to squirm, but I hold myself frozen. An uncalled-for movement would disappoint him, true, though it's not the worst that could happen. I'm so hot, too hot, that at the tiniest friction the floodgates would open to my orgasm and I'd come.

Panic rises when I see him lowering his head between my thighs, pushing them to the sides.

"Hudson, I—please, Sir," I mumble.

His hot breath falls on my slick opening, and I roll my eyes so high I'm sure I see my brain. My body is an electric field, living, breathing, and pulsating for *him*.

"Do. Not. Come, Avery."

He bites the inside of my thigh and I have to dig the heels of my feet to the floor in my attempt to control myself. The intense need to come and the order to hold on are two polar sensations that war inside of me, and I'm terrified of losing.

I pant, "Sir," and, "Please," again and again, pleading my one and only for the release he holds the key to.

"Give me your eyes." His fingers sink into the skin of my thighs, rubbing and massaging them higher, reaching my folds and parting them.

My throat is locked, teeth grating each other so hard it's audible. But I do as he says.

His eyes narrow when I lift my head an inch off the ground.

"The answer is no, little. You are not to come." Hudson's hot tongue laps at my pussy, swirling around my clit and I yell in the soundproofed room. "Screaming is allowed. Moving is not, nor is coming."

Harsh lips close around my nub, sucking it between his teeth. My body thrashes, my breaths are harsh gasps and my head thrashes to one side while my eyes remain fixated on him.

"I want you"—his tongue draws circles on my clit, and I levitate off the ground—"to be focused solely on obeying me."

"Yes." I inhale slowly, fighting the tide from having Hudson's fingers probe at my pussy. "Sir."

"I'm the one to protect you and care for you," he says, scraping my clit with his teeth and shoving his fingers inside me without a warning. "I take that job very seriously."

"I know, I know," I chant, but what do I really know at this stage?

Nothing, not even my own name. My entire existence hangs on a thread, and I grasp at straws, just not to come.

"That's it." His green eyes are sharp amid the blurry background of my vision. Then it becomes white hot, because his mouth is at my clit and his fingers pound into me, three at first, then four. "This is what I do. This is how I clear the negative voices that have no place in your mind."

I want to tell him my mind is currently blank, I want to beg him to let me let go. I want many things that I can't articulate, living in a void while my body detonates into space. I moan and scream, and I'm empty.

Hudson throws his jacket somewhere behind him, rolling up the sleeves of his shirt as he positions himself above my naked body. Accentuated veins course through his forearms, the muscles on them flexing as he places both hands on either side of my face.

"No one except you and me, blue." His dick slides up and down my clit, the tails of his dress shirt tickling my skin. "Say it."

For the longest moment, I stare at him. Googly eyes, open mouth, enamored and high and in such a state of nirvana, that I stop fighting my orgasm. I'm so lost that I barely exist.

"Blue." My avenging angel, my human, my solid rock, he bends down to kiss my nose, growling, "Say. It."

When he speaks up close like this, I hear him. "You and me."

"You and me, baby."

In one blinding rock of his hips, Hudson impales me with his unforgiving cock. He lingers there, his green eyes clashing into my blue ones and it's an absolute shock to the heart.

His words, too. "You may come."

My muscles clench, the buckles of my restraints clink at the sudden movement. I open my mouth to scream, but no sound leaves me. Hudson ignores my earth-shattering orgasm, pummeling into me in rough, deliberate strokes.

His cock swells inside me, stretching my walls, penetrating my soul and the buildup of another orgasm in me is inevitable. Hudson watches me grasping at the rope and clenching my teeth. He has to feel my hips locking him in, my soul about to leave my body.

He sets me free a second time, without torment or anticipation. But with love.

He whispers to my neck, "My forever love. Come again."

I do, and it's glorious, then made unearthly divine when my fiancé comes with me.

CHAPTER FOUR
Hudson

"Don't move," I warn.

Avery's and my faces are close. Her breaths are slow, trickling across my fingers then withering on my cheeks. There are many sensual aspects of our life together. Applying lipstick on her easily reaches the top five items of that list.

Nurturing her, taking care of her, and possessing her don't differ from fucking her tight little cunt or having her call me Sir. No other woman made me feel this way before, no other will ever again.

I kiss her forehead at the not-so-rare outburst of love.

We lean against my sofa, back in our evening wear and sitting on the Persian rug. The fire crackles in the fireplace, casting a warm light on Avery who's still floating between heaven and earth. Her shoulders sag, her body collapsed onto the sofa, her blue eyes round and grateful.

Finally, she's relaxed.

Although I hold her lipstick tube up to her lips, intent on coloring them pink, my mind wanders to other things. Or rather, it focuses on them.

My eyes roam her ruddy cheeks, puffed lips, her half-lidded eyes. Anything that might alert me to a crack in her mental well-being after the rough sex in the mirror room. I've taken the time to hug her, make her tea, and feed her small bites of the chocolate chip cookie she loves so much.

Despite doing all of that, I examine her one more time. We didn't just fuck. In that room, she opened up about something she hasn't communicated with me, something that's been bothering her. The weight of carrying that poison alone had to have been heavy, making another observation a necessity.

But my little seems to be fine.

A little rebellious, too.

"I am not moving." Her lips curve into a smile, contradicting her words.

We're half an hour late for the party, and I can't bring myself to care.

We wouldn't leave until she said so. Until she's ready.

"Your body doesn't."

A smirk snakes up my lips, unable to resist one around her. It took me a while to realize how my smiles became more frequent in her presence, but there's no denying it.

"Your lips, however…" My thumb grazes her bottom one. "Assuming we're not going for the Joker costume, you have to stay still."

"In all fairness, you did instruct me to part them." Her eyes glint in a challenge, fully awake at this point. "Make up your mind. Sir."

Because we're not really out of the aftercare period, Avery can be whomever she chooses to be. I accommodate each as they come, loving, adoring, and honoring her in every which way she comes to me.

Some days she's drained, collapsing in my arms and lets me rock her to sleep.

Others, she's chatty, asking me a million questions about my past or something she saw on the news. I answer her with honesty and patience, admiring her talkative side as well as her silent one.

On days she's neither this nor that, she's playful. These are rare, a handful of occasions where Avery reverts to the girl she is. She leaves Avery the marketing director or Avery who takes flogging and paddling and a dick up her ass somewhere behind her.

I wish they'd happen more often, for her young soul not to be buried under the responsibilities of adulthood.

This is why I never fail to play along, to encourage her.

"That mouth." I stroke a strand of her silky, brown hair, tucking it behind her ear.

"You love it."

"That, I do." My eyebrows climb up, encouraging her to do what I say next, "Here's me making up my mind. Part your lips."

"Okay." She complies, opening her mouth in the shape of an O.

Sharp pain strikes the inside of my cheek where my teeth lock on my flesh. I don't think I'll ever look at her gaping mouth and not want to shove my cock inside. Not after that first night, I smeared my precum all over it.

But it's not what we're doing now.

"That's it," I tell her as I dab the pink lipstick to the center of her bottom lip, then the top, before I begin to spread it to the corners. Once the lipstick is applied, I place the tube on the sofa in favor of her mascara.

"Eyes to the ceiling."

"Yes, Sir," she says, looking at the ceiling.

"We're not in a scene." Humor slips into my tone as I coat her lashes with the second layer of mascara like she asked me to.

"You're still my Sir. Always my Sir."

The world around me quiets. There's white noise in the air as if snow covers the room. I'm cognizant of the many roles I play in her life. It doesn't change the fact that there are goddamn fucking times where she says it and it hits me in a whole other way.

And after learning what I have today—how uncomfortable other people's opinions of her make her feel—I swear to myself I'll be that person for her. With a vengeance.

I'll be harsher than I ever have before, become an impenetrable shield to shut out anyone whom I perceive as a threat to my little. Today, and for the rest of our lives.

"You're right, baby." I lift myself to standing, helping her up to her feet. "I am."

The drive from my home in Outer Richmond, San Francisco, to the bar Whitlock rented for the Halloween party is about twenty minutes long. The place is located just outside of SoMa, near Avery's old apartment building where she used to live with her best friend, Jen.

My gaze trails to her as we pass the neighborhood, finding her lips turned up in a lazy smile.

It satisfies and bothers me in equal measure.

I place a hand on her thigh, massaging her through her dress. "Miss living here?"

There's a shift on the leather chair, of her turning to me. "You know I don't. More like reminiscing."

"About the days you lived with Jen?"

"Just Jen, in general."

The stop sign couldn't have come at a better time. I press the brakes and the Tesla stops in complete silence, turning to Avery.

My fiancée is a career woman through and through. She puts in endless hours of work in Pearl, her new workplace, willful in her pursuit to solidify her status at the office and in her battle to make sure no one dismisses her on account of her young age.

Her diligence is an admirable quality, one I recognize well from myself. It's the pillar of a person's reputation, and way I see it, it will pave Avery's way to being a VP in whichever company she chooses sooner, rather than later.

The problem is, it also comes with a hefty price tag. Her job and mine alike.

Neither of us is hardly at home, and when we are, we spend our remaining energy cozying up at home or fucking each other senseless.

Even a simple task like running off for a long weekend to meet her parents in Santa Barbara and then mine in L.A. took considerable work around our schedules.

Meeting her friends on top of everything? It hardly happens. A once-a-month thing, at best. Another roadblock I should've noticed sooner, as her fiancé and Sir alike. She's my responsibility to love, mine to look after.

All of that's about to change, now.

Car lights blink behind me, and I put the car in gear again, taking a right.

"Little blue."

She traces her thumb on the hollow space on my palm, between my thumb and index finger. "Yes?"

"Next week at work, before you even check your emails, mark your calendar as *out of office* on Wednesday from three p.m."

There are Halloween decorations on the storefronts, ghosts, knives, and fake fog. Pumpkins, skeletons, and scarecrows are staged at the entrances to the buildings, and people in all sorts of costumes walk the streets.

Avery isn't that impressed. She's suspicious. "For an hour?"

"Until the next day."

"Are we doing something special this Wednesday?" A second layer of suspicion seeps into her tone.

I refuse to waver, firming my grip on the wheel. "We are. And every Wednesday after that. We're going to be together, go out with your friends, go to a spa, or whatever you choose. That's our special something. Taking care of *yourself*, not Pearl."

"No." Avery's thumb ceases its stroking, her suspicion morphing into agitation. "I can't. I have my job, my responsibilities. You, of all people, should know how I have to work twice as hard to be respected. I can't just leave my employees every Wednesday and saunter out of there to have fun."

The answer is unacceptable, and I'm not dropping the conversation for Whitlock's party. It won't be a short one, knowing my fiancée and her dedication to her job. Working with Avery for three years and living with her for the past four months has taught me she won't back down when it comes to this.

What *she* still hasn't internalized about *me*, though, is that I won't ever back down when it comes to her well-being.

"It's not a discussion, Avery." I take a detour around the block, driving past the Hilton Hotel on Union Square. "Your psyche comes first. Your health comes first."

I slow when a group of twenty-somethings cross the street. My first thought is *they look happy*.

My second is *I need Avery to be that. To have what I didn't*. But I need to be smart about it too. In no way do I want to rob her of her sense of accomplishment.

An idea occurs to me.

Actually, two. One will have to wait.

The other, the one within an arm's reach, is happening right fucking now.

"Hudson, I understand your concern. But"—Avery grips the inside of Tesla as I speed up on Eddy Street—"Jeez, would you slow down?"

Rows of low buildings surround us, little lights shining from within them. I don't pay them or Avery's requests any mind.

"You can't tell me I can't work." Her voice sharpens around the edges.

On the next turn, I spin the wheel, taking a hard right and blending into Market Street, driving us toward the piers. "No one said you can't work."

"You did." Her eyes are on me, I can sense it. Defiant and strong. "It's only a matter of time until my boss would call me for a talk and what would I have to say in my defense?"

I look at her sideways, raising an eyebrow.

"What, indeed?" I ask, drawing her to the inevitable conclusion.

The sound of her gulp has to have been heard a mile away. "I can't tell her I was *ordered* to take care of myself."

"And therein lies another one of our problems." As we near our final destination, obviously *not* Whitlock's Halloween party, I slow the car.

"Our?"

"Yes, our."

My hand squeezes her thigh, and I light the blinker signaling to the right. The car slips past the gates of a parking lot, its innocuous appearance isn't raising any red flags for Avery.

Just how I want it to be. A surprise.

I smooth my hand up and down the soft chiffon skirt, yanking it up. Her cunt is hot and her thong is soaked in my palm when I cup it possessively. I say nothing, riding up to the second floor as if nothing's going on.

"Hudson," she whispers, her head making a soft thumping sound as it hits the back of the seat.

My name is meant to be a reproach, but her swaying hips and clenching thighs tell a different story. The story of submission. The story of giving in to the one who'll always have her best interests at heart. The story of *us*.

Her thong gives in easily when I push it to the side, her cunt sucking me in when I shove two fingers inside her. She's wet, her clit hard beneath the heel of my hand.

The fragrance of her sex replaces the clean scent of the car, quick gasps for air echoing over the classical music playing in the background.

"In case you haven't noticed, my love, we are one." I snap open both our seatbelts, grabbing one of her legs. "Watch your head."

Doing this long enough, she gets where we're headed. Avery balances herself by holding the side of her seat while I pull her by her thigh with extra force so she lies down.

"Your problems are mine." I angle my body to her, shoving the dress up her thighs to have her cunt bare to me. "Your happiness is the catalyst to my happiness."

Avery yells when I strong-arm her left knee down to her chest and thrust three fingers into her pussy. It's a beautiful sight, even in the harsh lights of the parking lot, made even more beautiful by the sounds of her juices as I push and shove my fingers.

"I'm in charge of those things. It's my job to see them done." My words are as full of intent as the glare I'm pinning her down with. "And believe me when I say that I have immediate and long-term solutions for one,"—I count, still ramming my fingers into her—"your happiness. Two, to continue our lifestyle without caring about others and without jeopardizing an inch of your career and accomplishments."

Her grunt of approval is all she can say. I'm not having it.

I take my hand out, slapping her clit. "Do you believe me when I say it?" I slap her a second time, relishing her scream. "That I'll fix it for you? That everything I do is for your own good?"

"Yes." Her head thrashes to the side, eyes remaining on me.

"Yes, what?"

I thrust three fingers back inside her, teasing her G spot using the pads of my fingers. Index finger, middle finger, ring finger, one after the other in a slow tormenting rhythm.

She squirms and grinds her ass on the chair to get more of me. I hold her knee down tighter. It's imperative she knows it to her bones.

"Yes, Sir."

"That's my good girl."

After getting the answer I wanted, I reward her with praise and resume pounding her cunt. The fingers of my free hand sink into her flesh, and her blue eyes darken.

She's close.

"We'll talk about it later, little." My thumb moves in intervals, drawing circles around her clit then pressing it down. "For tonight, though, I'm going to remind you what it's like to have fun in a place that accepts us. What we should aspire to have for the rest of our lives."

"Thank you," she breathes. Sweat coats her smooth forehead, her hips trying to lock me in place in her attempts to hold on. "Hudson, please."

"Please what?" I tap my wet thumb on her clit, feeling it harden beneath me.

"Please, let me come."

"Thanks for reminding me." I quirk an eyebrow, looking down at her. "That on top of everything else, your happiness, sadness, and problems, your orgasms are also *mine*."

Her entire body is a ball of energy ready to explode, coiled and fragile at the same time.

"Now, Avery."

Like the good girl she is, she comes.

CHAPTER FIVE
Avery

Hudson indicates that I interlace my arm with his on the elevator ride down. It doesn't escape me that we parked upstairs while the party is somewhere underground.

"Where are we going?" I peek at my tall fiancé.

The sharp lines of his jaw cast shadows on his strong cheeks, his chin is held up high. He looks as if we're smack in the middle of a gala for the rich and famous, not inside a slightly shaking, pee-scented elevator.

To the outside world, he might seem formidable, and he really is. But then he tilts his head down, and the curve of a smirk he saves just for me cuts through the ice, swathing me in warmth.

"You said you trusted me, didn't you?"

My head bobs, more from the jolt of the elevator car as we stop at minus three. Sultry music pours out behind opaque, black blinds, low red lights seeping from beneath them. I forget about the elevator instantly, curious to find out what lies behind them.

Hudson, on the contrary, is in no rush to get out. He calls for my attention by tracing his thumb along my heated cheek, ending his tour at my lips, and pulling on the bottom one.

"Don't overthink it. Let today happen, let yourself be young again."

"I—" I start, then think better of it and hush. I said I'd trust him, and I'm standing behind my word.

"You don't have to worry about a thing today, little. Or ever."

He bends lower to me, making my heart beat twice as fast when he's this close. His teeth bite into the lip he's holding, his free hand hitting the button to open the door as they slide close again.

"I'll keep you safe at all times." His lips drag across my skin up to my ear, and I forget how to breathe when his tongue laps at the shell. "Like I will for the rest of our lives."

He's there, and he's gone. I choke on air I can't fully expel out of my lungs, then land back into reality from the touch of Hudson's fingers as they slip into mine. We leave the elevator together, him strong and me a puddle of need, and as the elevator doors close behind us, we head together toward the darkness.

"Hudson." I tug his hand before he can open the curtains. "Have you been here before?"

"No." He squeezes my hand. "I heard about it through an old friend from college. I wanted to surprise you when the timing was right, which, as it seems, is the present moment."

Who is he or she? How do we know they sent us somewhere safe?

The questions I won't utter must be written all over my eyes because Hudson chuckles. "A friend who's been open about his kinks since we shared a room in the dorms. We've stayed in good contact since. He's reliable, don't worry."

The answer is more than satisfactory. Though I should've guessed that. "Okay."

"You ready?"

"Yes," I say. Ready for what, I don't know, but this is how trust works.

"Good girl." Hudson pats my head, his voice is a song of approval.

This gratifying hormonal reaction explodes in my tummy, and it's all I can do not to melt. My nipples harden all over again and my heart pounds fiercely for Hudson. Only ever for him.

He turns from me, pulling open the blinds and escorting me in. A girl with a high black ponytail and tight little black dress welcomes us with a bald bouncer three times her size standing ominously next to her.

Behind them, there's a door of frosted glass from one wall to another, where the orange Halloween-themed lights are visible. You can't see anything past that, can barely make out the music on the other side of the door.

It gives me a good idea as to where we are, and the anticipation is killing me.

"Welcome to Fly High Club, I'm Chrissy." She smiles with lips painted in a dark shade of red.

She's beautiful and friendly looking, though her tone accompanied by the bouncer behind her implies otherwise. They say *We won't hesitate to kick you out if you don't belong.*

"Burning star," Hudson replies without so much as a blink. "Rohan Davenport sent us."

"Rohan, huh?" Chrissy's polite smile morphs into a genuine one.

"Yes."

Through intrigued eyes, she studies us anew, her eyes lingering on my collar. "All right," she says, spinning on her heel and pushing in a black, secret door.

I shift on my feet, twirling a lock of my hair in my hand. Can a person be both thrilled and scared at the same time? Because I am. Very much.

"Little one." Hudson's voice soothes my nerves, and compliance is my only state of being during our wait for our hostess.

"There we go." Chrissy emerges from the back room, holding out two hangers. "I guessed your sizes, and I'm usually never wrong."

A plain black dress with thin straps hangs on one of them with a black and gold eye mask hanging at the top. On the other hand, there's a three-piece, all-black suit, a black dress shirt, and a black plastic full-face mask.

"These are for you. We had extra outfits of all sizes brought in, in case some patrons who haven't RSVPed would decide to drop by," she exclaims before we get to ask any questions. "The theme of the party tonight is that everyone's equal. It's a wonderful concept and"—she winks at me—"adds a ton to the mystery."

Hudson accepts both from her, handing me the one with the dress on it.

"Oh, and I'm going to need your phones. We value the privacy of our clients."

"Absolutely," Hudson says, collecting mine and handing both of them to her.

"Great. Once you enter," Chrissy continues her explanation, "you'll find two doors on either side, both are not attached to any gender. We built two so those who arrive as couples can split if they are interested in a sexy surprise for their partner. You can go in either one or go to change together, the choice is all yours."

"Thank you," Hudson says, and I thank her as well.

"You're most welcome. Have a spooky night." Chrissy does a little bow of her head, then nods to the bouncer.

The big guy moves to pull the glass door open, ushering us into the club.

A lot of work had been done on the place, and it looks impossibly rich and perfectly fitting for Halloween. The floor is covered in black slate, orange LED lights are hidden between the red brick walls to the ceiling and another frosted glass wall separates this room from another one.

The bar on the far left side of the room has a rich quality to it too. Three rows of liquor decorate the wall behind it, and a male bartender stands and pours a couple an orange, bubbly cocktails into martini glasses.

It's minimalistic and elegant and has sex plastered on the walls without having to spell it out.

The beat of *Lotus Flower* by Radiohead pounds through the speakers and Thom Yorke's voice reverberates into my core. I'm hot, my breasts are swollen, and I'm almost panting from the sensuality dripping out of every corner.

Electricity gathers at my back, warm, steady, and all-consuming.

Hudson.

He walks to stand behind me, his hand slithering forward to rest on my collar. I can feel his cock pressing to the small of my back, his hot breaths unfurling on my cheek.

With a strong shift of my torso, he twists us to the right. "After you."

But as I stand there, in love with my fiancé and enamored by the endless opportunities we can have together, I dare to disobey him. "I'm okay to change in different rooms."

His fingers pull on my collar, tilting my head to the right to meet his gaze. I read him, understanding he wants us to go in together for my sake, to give me a sense of security.

I thought I couldn't love him more.

I was wrong. So, very wrong.

"You sure?"

"Yes." I bite my bottom lip and his nostrils flare. "Sir."

His eyes are aimed at my mouth, but his teeth travel to my bare shoulder. He bites it while pulling me to him, his palm cutting out some of my air.

Like I care.

"Didn't want to ruin your lipstick." He trails kisses up, avoiding my collar on his way to my jaw. "Don't take too long."

"I won't."

Truth is, it won't take me any time at all. I don't tell him that though, nor do I tell him that even though tonight the costumes of everyone here are supposed to be the same, I'm adding a touch of my own.

Tonight, I'm going to be a brat.

CHAPTER SIX
Avery

I'm out of my chiffon gown in less than a minute. I slip on the black dress Chrissy handed me, wriggling into it over my navy-blue strapless bra and matching thong. It fits surprisingly well, tight but not suffocating, snug enough to help push my breasts high up without spilling over the fabric.

The music from the club blares into the dressing room. *Bury a Friend* by Billie Eilish and the prospect of the games I'm about to play with Hudson break a chill down my spine. I ignore it, focusing on the task at hand, heading to the wall-to-wall mirror on one side of the room.

It's lit by orange LED light fixtures, though their tone is warmer here, leaning toward a soft combination of orange and yellow rather than bright orange. Along the mirror, there's a black slate bar to match the floor, and on top of it is exactly what I've been looking for—tissue boxes.

I hurry to wipe off my pink lipstick when luck strikes a second time. A tall, blonde girl emerges from one of the dressing rooms, her hair pinned up high in a carefully constructed bun with a spare hairband on her wrist.

"Hi." I turn to her, looking up. "Would you mind sparing me your extra hairband?"

She eyes me up and down, her tongue flicking out to graze her bottom lip. Her gaze is heated, and she is gorgeous, but there's only one man I'm committed to, one person I'll love to the day I die.

"Sure." She tugs it off her wrist, handing it over to me. "Nothing else?"

My lack of experience is embarrassing, and I'm grateful to have the surrounding in shades of pink and red to cover my blush. "You're a beautiful woman."

Words fail me, so I let my collar speak for me, angling my chin higher to show it.

No other possession I have or will have matches the meaning it holds in my life.

The day Hudson brought it home, my insides melted then galloped and twisted like lava erupting in my belly. This love declaration, the finality of his ownership of me— no diamond ring could ever come close. Which is why I might've forgotten my ring, but I'll never, ever forget *this*.

I even remember the words he told me as he put it on that Saturday night when it was just us in our living room.

He lit what looked like a million jasmine-scented candles and spread them across the dark living room, wore a black suit, and picked out a white maxi boho dress for me. I had no idea what he had in mind, but the second my eyes laid on the lace collar, I didn't need to be told what was going on.

I just knew.

"Avery Myers."

"Soon to be Kent."

He hiked an eyebrow up, and I quieted, eager to please him.

"Soon, indeed. Until then, until we take our vows under the altar, I wanted to show you just how mine *you are." He cleared his throat, his pause and hesitation as uncharacteristic as vanilla sex is between us. "It's no secret that I've loved you for years. It's no secret that I think the world of you, that without you, life has no meaning. Food loses its taste when you're not around, music lacks any sort of rhythm. You take up every minute of my every day, little, and if there's one thing I regret in our relationship is not following my heart sooner."*

At this point I was crying. Big, fat, embarrassing, ugly tears.

He walked up to me, plucked out a tissue from a box on our coffee table, and wiped my cheeks so carefully, I started bawling again.

"Let me finish, love." He offered me a sad and loving smile, his stern side neglected, if only for today. "It ruins me to see you cry."

I nodded, doing as he said. I always tried to satisfy him, always.

His eyes grew tender, pleased. "That's my good girl."

I nodded some more. I couldn't imagine talking unless I wanted to start crying again.

"This collar,"—he held it up between us, dangling on his palm as it faced up, and I placed my own hand on top of it—"symbolizes not just my ownership of you, but yours of me as well. I vow to be the best partner I can be for you, to love, nurture and take care of you, my little blue. It's the testimonial to our all-powerful bond, to our unbreakable connection. Do you accept it?"

"Can I..." I ground my teeth, holding on so fucking tight to my tears. "Can I say a few words too?"

His thumb stroked the outside of my palm, his voice laced with amusement. "Could it start by you saying 'I do'?"

"Oh my gosh." I huffed a watery laugh. "Of course, I do."

Hudson leaned in, smashing our hands into our chests. He cupped the back of my head and kissed my forehead, talking into my skin. "Then yes, you may."

"I love you," I blurted out when he returned to his place. "I love you, your serious expressions and the smiles that hide behind them. I love that you save them for me, a lot. I love how strong you are, inside and out. There's nothing about you that I don't love, from how you move me around like a rag doll or how you bathe me so tenderly, like I might break. I love..." I sniffed, my fingers flexing on his. "I love that you exist. And I love that

you found me. Would you do me the honor of putting this collar on me?"

He did. It was tender and powerful and perfect in every sense of the word.

"I see." The tall lady peruses my collar in her black eyes while I pin my hair up in a messy bun. Her look changed from interested to appalled a short moment later when I took it off and stuffed it in my bra.

"Why would you do that?"

My face is lit from the inside as I try to explain myself. "I want to hide and see how long it takes for him to find me."

The tall lady pauses, her eyes widening. Then she laughs. "That's one interesting game. Wish I would've thought about it."

"Thanks, gotta go." I tie my mask around my head in rushed movements. "Sorry if I'm being rude. I have to get out before he does, otherwise, I did all of this for nothing."

"You're good," she says. "My name's Sheila, by the way."

"Avery!" I wave, holding my dress up and running out of the room, the door shutting behind me.

Hudson isn't there, thankfully. Truth is, no one is, not even at the bar.

I power walk toward the bartender, speaking before he can offer me anything to drink. "Hey, so my fiancé will be out of the dressing rooms any moment now. Tall, dark-blond hair, green eyes."

"Okay…"

"Tell him I went inside. I don't want him to worry or anything." I skate my eyes to the door to the dressing room, knowing my time is limited. "Don't tell him that my hair is up though."

The bartender, who has probably seen just about anything and everything, remains unperturbed. "Sure thing. Happy Halloween."

"Thanks, you too."

With my plan intact, I march to the frosted door, pull it open, and walk inside.

The room I enter is more of a hanger than anything. The design here is similar to the entrance area, yet isn't the same. The walls here aren't brick, but painted in black. There's a thick layer of white smoke rising from the floor, the music is far louder and the lights are dimmer.

Although it doesn't hinder my ability to see anything. I move through the people scattered around the hangar, curious about my surroundings while sticking to my mission of finding a hiding place.

It doesn't take me long to locate several of them. On either side of the space, there are separated into intimate alcoves where patrons sit or lie down on floor cushions. They're in groups of twos and threes or more, in every position one can think of.

Dampness pools at my center from watching a woman sucking off a man while another woman pegs her from behind. I continue walking, getting even wetter at the view of shadows of two long-haired women eating each other out, of a man sucking and licking a woman's toe.

So many of them. I clench my thighs, needing Hudson yesterday.

Upon a closer look, I see all of the women are still wearing their masks, contrary to the men—those who use their mouths. The clothes either stay on them or are thrown around the alcoves.

Shadows and scents of tits and cunts and hard cocks overcome me, tightening their hold on me the more I stare.

The whole scenery is incredibly hot, and as I weave my way through, I let my imagination run wild. In my mind's eye, I picture Hudson taking me into one of these alcoves, tearing off my dress, punishing me without a shred of mercy for misbehaving.

He won't approve of me choosing a trick instead of a treat, and for once, I'm consciously and actively seeking his dissatisfaction.

Suddenly, the air is sucked out of my lungs, my heart thrumming in a familiar beat.

Hudson is here.

No, not him, not really. From the energy reverberating through me and without so much as a glance in his direction, I recognize him for what he is.

He's Sir.

When I do look, my suspicions are verified. Even wearing the mask, I pinpoint him from the rest. His confident posture, the veins cording his neck, his elegantly disheveled hair. He spins his head slowly, scanning the room for me.

The thrill I get out of having him ignore everyone else, of him searching for me, edges me to rebel harder, dreaming of my punishing reward. I stick around a second longer, until his gaze trails over to where I'm standing, and then I turn away.

I'm elegant in my twirl, acting as though I wasn't just caught by him. There's space for me to navigate past the people toward the end of the room, and my dress swishes on the smoky floor as I do so.

My eyes lock on a deserted alcove. I cut through the straight path I walked in, heading to where I'd want Hudson to find me. Where I want him to punish me, to slap my ass raw and bite my breasts until the skin breaks, and there isn't a part of me that isn't black or blue or red.

Until he's satisfied that I'm his good girl again.

I slip my sandals off, positioning myself behind the alcove. One of my hands clings to the side wall, my head peeking out to look for him. He strides forward, his gait determined, his eyes constantly searching.

With my last shred of willpower, I hold myself from reaching between my thighs where the ache is unbearable. I long for Hudson, love him, crave him.

Need him.

He shifts his attention to the other side, and I bite my lips in anticipation as he twists back to where I'm hiding. But he can't see me anymore. Not because I reverted into the alcove, not because I'm hiding.

A dark-haired man with broad shoulders faces me, hiding my line of view of my fiancé. "Waiting for someone?"

"Yes," I say, anxious for him to move away.

"Could that person be me?" He inches a step forward, opening his fly.

"No," is all my dry mouth can muster.

Smidgens of worry eat at my insides. I understand this is a sex club. While I haven't been to one ever, I'm aware that coming on hard could be expected. Some people like it and that's okay. I love the freedom it offers, the sexual liberation.

But it's not working for me. I need to draw my boundaries, and I'm so stuck between stunned and petrified that I can't.

The man takes another step, and in my terror, not one other syllable comes out of my throat. I need to call Hudson, but I can't. I need him to find me, but I'm starting to realize he might not.

The man, ignorant or enjoying my terror, rubs his fully erect cock. He tears the mask off my face and doesn't care that I gasp, reaching out to cup the side of my neck, not stopping to jack off again and again.

I want to scream. I want to slap him. I want to turn and run home.

"Why don't you be a good girl and get down on your—"

He doesn't get to finish his sentence, though. Nor does he get to touch me again.

Hudson grabs him by the neck, twisting him to face green eyes that shine bright even behind the shadows of his mask.

"Why don't *you* back. The fuck. Off her."

CHAPTER SEVEN
Hudson

I recognized Avery from across the room. Her energy is unparalleled, a unique concoction created exclusively for me. She didn't have to pin her hair up, wipe off her makeup, or remove her collar to hide from me.

We're too deeply connected that no matter what mask my fiancée has on, I will always find her. It will never take me over a split second, no matter where we are, no matter how many other people are there.

She's mine. Nothing will ever change that.

The reason I haven't gotten to her sooner was to please her. I could tell she enjoyed the chase, that she liked the mystery, the idea of running and hiding in the crowd. That it would taste that much sweeter in her mouth when I had my hands on her.

When I took her and punished her, loved her like I had four months ago.

Like I haven't, not completely like I used to or what we read about. The realization is another blow for tonight, of something I've missed, something Avery's not communicating with me.

She needs my hard side more often. The tenderness of her, the cotton candy woman who lives with me, softens my heart. I can't stay indifferent or somber to the late-night dinners she fixes for me, to the coffee on her knees in the mornings, to her little pecks while we're watching television.

She deserves the rough man I've always been to her throughout our working years together, during the beginning of our relationship. Hell, I deserve it, to be the person she enables me to be—myself.

It's not that I'll love her less. Doesn't even suggest I'll treat her with any less respect than I have since the first day her blue eyes fluttered at me at Whitlock, from when her pretty little smile locked me to her by chains.

I couldn't, even if I wanted to.

But I will steer this ship back to where we both belong.

First, though, I have to deal with the piece of human trash I'm holding.

"Who the hell are you?" The man who assaulted Avery dares to speak anything other than an apology.

I knew where I was taking her. The people here can look at her, admire her. In this place, I'll even allow a person to stand in the distance and jerk off on her.

What they cannot, will not do, is touch her.

She's mine. And she's scared shitless. It's the first time I've seen Avery this helpless, stunned into silence with her eyes wide and her palm flat against her chest.

Even if she weren't mine, there isn't a *no* more blatant than that. No man should ever violate a woman or intimidate her just because he fucking can.

My hand is at his throat, my eyes burning into his. I could say a million things that would represent my relationship with Avery. I'm her lover, fiancé, her Sir.

They're all inaccurate though. Halfway explanations.

There's only one truth, standing high above the rest.

"She belongs to me." I snarl though he can't see it behind my mask. "Avery. Is. Mine."

"You realize where you're at, man?" His hands fumble for his pants, tucking his dick away. "Kinda expected."

People gather around us. I see them out of the corner of my eye, sense them at my back. Then I gaze behind the masked asshole's face and I see the woman whom I put on a pedestal above the rest of the world.

Her gaze is expectant. They communicate what I know: being this cocky, this uncaring of her evident fear, this can't be his first offense.

I bring his ear to my mouth. "Do not call me 'man.' And I don't believe they have *assault* on the menu."

A finger taps on my shoulder, hard. "We'll take it from here, sir."

I turn around, not letting go of the guy. The mountain of a bouncer waits for me, behind him someone who could very well be his twin.

"We saw what went down on the CCTV." His frame is bigger, wider than mine, and there's an apology in his voice. At least someone here has the decency to. "We came here as fast as we could. I'm sorry it wasn't faster."

His words aren't enough to quell the fire burning inside me. However, there are other considerations. Avery and I are not finished with what we came here for. Not even close.

The guy stumbles forward when I release him to the hold of the bodyguard.

"Thank you, and we apologize. This is the last he'll step foot in here."

I nod once, patting down the suit jacket they gave me at the entrance. The expensive fabric smooths beneath my palms, and so is the ball of red-hot blazing anger behind my eyes. It's crucial to have it wither and die.

I will not, under any circumstance, address or touch Avery when I'm not fully in control of myself. Will never get into a scene with her when I'm mad or angry.

"Hudson?" she says to my back.

There's still wavering in her voice, and I fucking hate that this sorry excuse for a man planted it in her.
Breathe.

Ten seconds pass. I count down, patient and trusting the process. The heat shifts in my chest, the temperatures drop. The familiar, icy chill resumes its place in my mind, and that's when I take off the mask, throw it to the floor, and turn to her.

My brow is furrowed, my lips pulled into a tight line. I'm the man I was born to be, the Sir she fell in love with. "Little blue."

"I'm so sorry for running off." Avery bows her head, her gaze trained at my chin, not my eyes.

Heat pulses right through me again. This time, though, rage doesn't fuel it. Arousal does. My cock is rock hard, my hands itching to touch Avery every-fucking-where.

"Come here." I'm stern and unyielding.

She walks the few short steps necessary for her to reach me. The dress flows around her and I notice she's barefoot. One less item to take down.

Once she's closer, words of apology fumble out of her mouth. "I'm sorry I didn't think this through, I wanted this to be fun for us and I've ruined it. I ruined everything."

"Where is your collar?"

Her rambling stops, and she sniffles.

"Don't." I place a finger under her chin, raising her head. Watery blue eyes with orange gleams stare at me. "I'm not mad. Not about that."

"About what then?"

"Don't make me repeat myself." There are still eyes on us. I ignore them.

She shoves a shaky hand into the front of her dress, taking out the lace and leather collar I gave her as a symbol of our commitment. Weddings are formal, intended for the outside world. This collar, however, was all us.

"I—" she starts.

Instead of kissing her like I want to, I put a finger in her mouth. There'll be time for taking her lips later. Now, I'm working on reclaiming her heart.

"Not another word." I pull at the collar and she gives it to me. I tower over her, occupying her space. "Turn around."

She does, moving her hair to the side to expose her neck. Its soft curve and the dimness of the club send me to the night I put it on her. How a sick part of me loved it so fucking much I wanted to ink its pattern into her skin, and how I obliterated that idea in a second.

Ink wouldn't be a conscious choice. She wouldn't have to take off the ink in the shower, wouldn't have a say on whether to put it on or not day in, day out.

With the collar, she has a choice. And she always chooses us.

I wrap the fabric around her neck, tugging on it to draw her closer. My cheek presses to hers, my breath is hot at her ear. "You've been bad."

"I know. I'm so sorry."

"You're not apologizing for the right thing." I return to finish fastening the buckle on the collar, then release the locks of hair I love to run my hands through as much as I love pulling on them. "I thought we talked about it earlier this evening. However, I'm more than willing to remind you what you forgot. Turn back to me."

She complies, her arms straight and hands crossed in front of her. "What should I be apologizing for, Sir?"

My index finger runs down her temple, her jaw, her sternum. "What did I ask you today, back home?"

She doesn't linger in giving me my answer. "To tell you the truth."

"Correct." I flip my finger, my knuckle grazing her tenderly. Her reward. "So, what do you have to be sorry for?"

"For not communicating. For not telling you what I want."

I twist her in my arms so her back is to me. Many patrons of the club stand in half a circle around us, witnessing our interaction. Their curiosity and arousal overflow from them even from behind their masks, even in the darkness.

A few people have their hands down their underwear. They pleasure themselves to the beat of whatever sultry song they have in the background, waiting to see my next move.

"That's very good." I bite her earlobe and she yelps.

My hand slides to the front of her body, grabbing a fistful of her skirt and bunching the fabric up her hips. The thin lace of her soaked thong tears at the slightest pull, the falling to the floor.

The crowd around us grows, becoming more restless. Some of them pair up, like the man to my right who shoves a woman to her knees to have her suck him off while he watches us.

There's even a trio in front of us, two women licking and sucking and fondling the third woman in the middle. They yank her breasts out, pleasure her pussy, and all the while their attention is dead set on Avery and me.

Avery's pulse dances wildly beneath the palm I have plastered on her chest. "You like having them watch you?"

"I—"

I angle her body forward, shoving two fingers into her pussy. "Only the truth."

She turns her head slightly to me. "I like it. I like that you claim me in front of them. I like how I'm not afraid of them because no one can touch me when you're here."

And here it is. What she wanted from me. Why she grinned when I promised her safety at the Whitlock party, the reason behind her sudden need to be a brat.

So I can prove to her how she's not only mine, but she's my little one.

My good little girl.

"I'm proud of you."

She moans, letting her head drop to my shoulder. I'm not sure if it's the thumb I add to massage her clit or the praise. It carries little weight, which of the two it really is.

"You're still going to have to be punished."

"I know."

"For hiding things from me. For not communicating like we promised to one another."

"I know."

I remove my fingers out of her pussy, pinching her clit and tweaking it. "Know, what?"

"I know, Sir."

"That's my girl."

My eyes scour for the CCTV cameras. I locate the one nearest to us and cross my fingers, the hand gesture Rohan instructed me to use in case I needed anything from the staff.

While we wait, I keep stroking her, stopping the second Avery's walls start clenching around me. "Now, how is it ever going to be remotely close to a punishment if I let you come?"

CHAPTER EIGHT

Avery

While Hudson and I wait for the staff of the club to get him a chair and a—marker? I think I heard him say along with a few other things—my fiancé does his absolute worst.

I don't ask him why he turned us from them, but he answers anyway.

"This is all on you, little, this punishment." His stubble tickles my jaw as he speaks, his voice commanding. "You're not getting any encouragement, no support. Your orgasm, for the time being, is for me to control and for me to witness."

My bare breast rests in his palm, my pussy at his complete and utter mercy.

"You want to learn how to be my good girl the hard way?" He adds another finger, four now, to pummel in and out of me. "You got it."

"Hudson, please." I almost cry out when his thumb dives deep into me, collecting dampness, and runs up to rub my clit in torturous slow circles.

"Please what?"

He presses his thumb hard against my clit, dragging the hard, sensitive flesh to the side. My right hand flings up to wrap around his neck, and the sounds emanating from my chest couldn't possibly be described as anything remotely human.

There are multiple facets to what makes holding back such a beautiful practice, in all its cruelty. The end result, for one, cannot be described as an orgasm. It's an assault of the senses, the thief of your breath, an invisible tie draped around your eyes because the pleasure is so exquisite, it blinds you.

Then that's where Hudson comes in. Being this submissive is like I've become an empty vase, and the power he exerts on me is as if someone pours water into my soul. He fills it to the brim, making me whole every day anew.

Even when he doesn't murmur *Good girl* and *You're taking this punishment so well* continuously in my ear, I feel it. And I know, I absolutely know, that through the strength he lends me by holding me upright, through his pounding heart and throbbing cock at my back, that I can do it.

I can please him.

I hold on to this orgasm with dear life.

"Nothing, Sir."

"Very good, little."

"Thank you."

"Mr. Kent." A voice booms at our backs, trying to be heard over the music. "We brought you what you asked for."

Hudson's teeth sink into my shoulder one final time, then he releases me to address the staff member. I do the same.

"Thank you."

My fiancé puts something that resembles a thin belt into the inside pocket of his suit jacket, and the marker I suspected he asked into his breast pocket. He approaches me, holding the back of a wooden chair, then kicks the floor cushions unceremoniously outside of our alcove.

I follow his moves like a love-sick puppy. The veins on his hand are accentuated by his strong grip on the chair, yet his face is impassive and cold as they come.

The song in the background could be roaring lions for all I care; the people are Lego figurines. There's only Hudson, the man who'll tell me what I can do to make up for not telling him what bothered me.

He's right to be upset. Relationships rely on honesty, and ours ten times more.

I know for certain Hudson will never spank me more than I can take, will never give me false praise, and will always, always be there for the aftercare.

He, in turn, knows that I'll say my safeword when our scene gets to be too much, that I'll speak my mind if I consider one of his demands to be wrong. He also knows—or at least he believed he did—that I'll tell him what bothers me so he can fix it, uphold his vow to me.

I've been stupid not to do it. But what's done is done. And this is my chance to learn from it.

He sits down on the chair, leaning back and spreading his knees. His thumb rubs across his bottom lip, looking me up and down. He has this bored stare in his eyes, a bit of a snarl on his lips. It's an indication he's keeping his emotions in check, his feelings under lock and key.

What usually follows is a one-word command, such as *strip*, *kneel*, or *beg*. Sometimes as long as *Open your legs*.

I wait for either.

And I wait. And wait. And wait.

Nothing.

There are murmurs in the background, the club patrons' excited voices telling me they've come closer. They're air. They're invisible.

Only Hudson.

Maybe he wants me to do something, to show what I'm willing to do for his forgiveness. I opt for the other strap of my dress, the one he didn't shove down my arm. My eyes cast to him, for his approval, as my thumb slides beneath it.

"No." He adds a shake of his head to the word he shoots at me.

I try the other command that comes to mind. My knees begin their descent to the floor, and then—

"No."

Exhilaration and disappointment wage a war inside my heart. For the four months we've lived together he's never slipped out of his Dom role, but he's been more lenient toward me. Like he grants me his forgiveness when I get too swamped at work that I forget our lunch hour checkup.

Of course, I'm not looking to be punished every time. I am a human, flaws and all. But how I love it when he shows me that he cares enough to take his precious time to consider what would be the best course of action for *us*.

Many minutes pass where I'm standing there with arousal dripping down my thigh and heavy breasts aching to be touched.

How many? No idea.

I just know when it's over.

"Come here." He beckons me to him.

My feet tread the cold slate floor until my toes are an inch from his shoes.

"On my lap."

At the half step I take to move to stand between his legs, he raises a hand to stop me.

"*Sitting* on my lap is for when you've been good." He cocks an eyebrow. "You think you are? You think you've earned it, little one?"

"No." I drop my eyes to the floor, wringing my hands.

"That's right." He leans a little further into his chair. "Take off my belt."

A woman moans behind us as I bend down to the buckle of the black leather belt, a man comes hard enough that I hear his guttural cry.

My fingers shake as adrenaline courses through my body. For all my doubts about our future, Hudson never had a single one.

He's taken me here, to a gathering of hot bodies and sexy scenarios to not simply make me feel like I belong somewhere. Hudson, once he was onto me and what I've been hiding, proves through actions how he'd stop at nothing in his pursuit to make me happy.

I don't question for a second his decision to whip my butt in front of dozens of unfamiliar eyes. I don't and won't question any of his decisions ever again.

The leather makes a whooshing sound as the belt the club must've given him slips out of the belt loops. My eyes remain low, honed in on his stomach and lap, on the outline of his erect cock.

Hudson breaks me out of my trance, flipping his palm to face up. "Give it to me."

Wordlessly, I do.

He accepts it, tapping it on his lap. A wave of desire has my knees buckling, and my legs shake. Hudson curls his long fingers all the way around my bicep, handling me in controlled force into his lap.

I'm lying on my stomach, gazing up to see the wall of the alcove in front of me.

Then, in the span of a split second, my skirt is being hiked up my hips and the cold leather hits me hard. It's a hard, intentional blow, and my skin feels like it's been sliced where Hudson spanked me.

"I'm going to spank you eleven times, Avery, on top of this one." His gaze appears in my blurred line of vision, where the lust for him consumes me whole. "Every slap will stand for every letter of the sentence you're about to spell. It's crucial you have it tattooed in your brain, the words and their profound meaning. This exercise will ensure that you won't forget."

My muscles clench to subdue my tremors, my eyes seeking Hudson's for his explanation. I'm quiet, observant, expecting.

He leans down, clearing hair out of my face. "Each time my belt connects with your body, you will spell—scream the words *You are my Sir* for me. Understood?"

Tears rise to my eyes, but it's not from pain or humiliation. They rise out of pure excitement, and I've never been more ready for anything in my entire life.

His stern gaze focuses me somewhat back into the here and now. "Use your words."

"Yes, Sir."

"Let me hear your safeword."

"Whitlock."

"Good."

He straightens in his chair. The world slows, just before Hudson swerves our existence into highway 101.

Smack!

My right bottom, the one closest to him, stings, burns, and hurts, and is a stark reminder of my devotion to Hudson.

"Y!"

The right one gets another slap. "O!"

"Louder," he instructs. A third one to my right. My eyes roll in pain, tears streaming down my cheeks, dripping to the floor. "U!"

His fingers are pushed into my cunt, his lips at my ear. "Do not come."

I whimper in agreement, though it's taking every last ounce of energy to comply. One of my dangling hands grips his calf in anticipation of the hellfire of slaps I know are just around the corner.

With each one of them, as he instructed, I scream out a letter. I would've screamed either way, if I'm being honest. Between being spanked repeatedly on my ass and inner thighs and having my swollen cunt pleasured to the point of oblivion, it's really all I can do.

When he's done, Hudson massages my ass and thighs in amorous, gentle strokes. He helps me sit in his lap, careful so my butt cheeks are in the air to avoid pain. My hands fling around his neck, and he supports me by having his arm on my back.

Green, potent eyes stare down at me, and I get lost in them and his words. "I can't tell you how proud I am."

My clit and my heart are equally swollen. "Thank you."

His thumb strokes my cheek. "Do you get it now?"

"I do."

"In case you ever forget." He levels his eyes with me. "You ask me. Anything you ever need, you ask me for it."

"Yes, Sir."

"Do you want to come?"

"Please."

His lips curve into a smirk. Hudson drives his fingers inside me and I clench around him and come so hard, my ears still ring seconds later.

He kisses my lips hard, and even without his fingers inside me, I come apart at his hold again.

His smile slants across my lips, "This is where the fun part starts."

CHAPTER NINE
Hudson

Avery and I leave the comfort of the chair. My hands, arms, and legs guide and support her movements until we're both on our feet.

My eyes skim my little with her one tit out and her darkened cheeks and wild hair. She's strong, but she's feeble. She's her own person, and she's mine.

I look at her downcast eyes and clasped hands in front of her, at her surrender. I look at her, and I love her. I look at her, hard and well with all those people around us and I know with every fiber of my being there will never be any other.

The question that's been running over in my head for the past two months, the one she forced me to reconsider today without knowing so, isn't a question anymore. It's a decision. There's a finality to it, in a place where hesitation ceases to exist. And I will ask her to agree to it.

After.

"Little one," I call her name, using the voice that binds her to me.

Two shining diamonds peek at me under a thick set of lashes. "Sir?"

There's a shift in the air around us. I glance at the onlooking spectators. They've grown in number, and some took the liberty to get too close to our alcove. My gaze holds not an ounce of kindness, my raised palm in a *stop* gesture leaves no room for interpretation.

They cease their advances. They still touch, stroke, suck, and ram into each other, but they will not violate what's mine.

"Your other breast." As they stop, I revert my attention to her. "Take it out."

Her delicate fingers wrap around the fabric of the dress, tugging it down, yanking her bra down with it.

My innate possessiveness dictates my next moves. I palm her breast, clench my fist around it and bring it to my lips. My open mouth hovers over her erect nipple, my other arm circles her waist and thrusts her into my cock.

"Who do you belong to?"

"You."

"That's correct."

She doesn't arch her back, isn't asking for more. She's my obedient, subdued little girl again. I reward her with a slow circle of my tongue around her areola, ending it with the tip of my tongue at her nipple.

Goosebumps spread across her chest, and I feel her moans down to my very core. I'm so hard, want her so badly that I can't think straight.

And I need to.

In one swift motion, I unbutton my pants, lowering the zipper in one push. I grab Avery's wrist, shoving it into my pants. The friction restores some of my sanity. That, and how well she takes care of me.

"Tell me your safeword," I repeat my request, adamant to make absolutely sure it's at her disposal.

"Whitlock." Her thumb grazes a drop of precum, rubbing it over my swollen head.

My teeth bite hard into her breast, and she screams. "Very good."

Slowly, I make my way up her chest, talking to her in intervals as I suck on the soft area between her neck and shoulder. "So this is how it's going to play out. We're going to get into the Halloween spirit, take on new roles while still being us."

"Okay." Her head inclines a little to the side, engulfing me with her hair and her scent.

"Harder." I thrust my groin into her, and she complies, pumping my dick inside my boxers.

"You will be my pet for the night." My fingers dent her sensitive ass, but the only sound coming out of her is more of those moans. "I will be your owner. And we're going to make a fucking spectacle out of it so everyone here knows you're mine. Got it?"

"Y—yes." She frees my cock out of my boxers, angling the head to her clit and rubbing it against the fabric of her dress.

I'll lose myself a hundred times over when I finally fuck her tonight.

"Enough." I pull back, tucking myself and zipping up with one hand, grabbing her chin with the other. "You dirty little whore. You want my cock?"

Avery's lips are dry, and she swallows what has to be air. "Please."

"Stand still." My focus is on her as I shove my hand into my breast pocket and take out the marker.

I angle my chin up. "Tilt your head back." When she does, I pop open the marker's cap, letting it fall to the floor. The pads of my fingers ghost along her collarbone, her nipples, below her breast.

On my canvas.

In bold black letters, I write *PROPERTY OF HUDSON KENT* on her chest.

Holding a finger to her chin, I apply pressure on it to lower it in place. "Want me to tell you what I wrote on your body?"

"I felt it." The orange of the club's lights is reflected in her eyes. She's beautiful, feline, the epitome of sex. "I really am. Master."

I stifle a growl, taking a step back to create distance between us. "This is the last you'll speak tonight until I tell you otherwise."

She nods. Her immediate obedience satisfies me to no end.

"On your hands and knees, little blue."

Her knees hit the slate floor first, her palms second. They disappear into the thick layer of white smoke, and she cranes her neck, waiting for further instructions.

I'll drive my car off the Golden Gate Bridge before saying there's a sight more beautiful than Avery's naked body. That, and having her hair drape to cover her front. The glimpses of her, the promise in it, affect me the same way as her being full-frontal would.

"So perfect, expecting her owner's commands." I walk until my shoe is parallel to her palm. I stroke the top of her head twice, then pet it.

A slow, seductive cover of *House of the Rising Sun* plays in the background, slow and sensual, much like my movements. Out of my pocket, I take out the vibrator I carry on me on the rare occasions we go out. The one and only vibrator we have, the one I used to pleasure her for the first time four months ago on the top of my car.

"You see that?" My voice is loud, overheard above the music drifting through the speakers and the others' moans and grunts and cries as they pleasure themselves or come.

Avery nods, eyes twinkling. She ignores the world around us, her focus is aimed at her Master.

"Want me to use it on you?"

She nods, then does something I didn't see coming. Something that sends a pulse of heat straight to my crotch, making me want to fist her hair and fuck her mouth until my sperm shoots straight down her throat.

Avery lifts her hand like a dog does a paw.

"That's a very good girl." The smirk on my face is inevitable. "We're playing a different game tonight. You want me to make you come with it, you're gonna have to fetch."

Her hungry eyes are wide.

Mine too.

I check one last time where our clear perimeter ends and raise my hand.

Then toss it over there.

CHAPTER TEN
Avery

An insidious kind of arousal courses beneath my skin, swarming my heart and overtaking it in its darkness. This isn't like any other I've experienced in the past, not even when Hudson fucked me in our old office over the weekend.

On all accounts, I should feel humiliated on my hands and knees. I should feel degraded and less than when he throws me the vibrator, telling me to fetch it.

I should, and many others probably would've.

And yet I don't.

With love as strong as ours and a bond more powerful than life itself, there's no room for anything except elation.

By calling me his pet and treating me as one, Hudson absolves me of my human responsibilities. The stress at work, the nagging thoughts at the back of my head of what people would say, they disintegrate into ashes when I'm at his feet.

I'm free in ways I had no idea I could be. I'm loved in ways no sonnet can describe.

His eyes glower at me from above, and I glare back, mesmerized.

Hudson bends his knees, just enough for this tall man of mine to reach my jaw and grab it. "In our four months together, have you ever heard me say I approve of you making me wait?"

I pinch my lips tight, shaking my head.

His release is forceful, thrusting my head to the side. "Then on with it."

The effort to subdue my moan is immeasurable. Through the pain of my beaten ass and thighs and my bare knees connecting with the floor, I do. Driven by the sheer force of wanting to please him, I turn to move in the direction where he tossed the vibrator.

I want to go there, and yet I can't. I see them. After minutes of being encapsulated inside Hudson's and my own little universe, I see their faces. Most of them have taken off their masks, and they're real people now, with real eyes looking at me act like a dog.

The vibrator isn't visible under the cloud of smoke. It could be close to them, they could outstretch their arm and Hudson would be too far back. They could grab me.

My collar spins around my neck. A pull and a *click* sound follow.

"I'll never ask you for anything you can't handle." Hudson's rough voice speaks in my ear. *The* voice. *His* voice. "You will do it, little, have no doubts about it. We'll go together at first, show them that not one fucking person is allowed to ever lay a finger on you."

Tears of gratitude gloss my eyes, and I shift my gaze to my owner. He stands up, self-assured as always, scanning the crowd to see if someone would dare challenge him. None of them do, not even me when I notice what the source of the clicking sound I heard was.

Rolled around Hudson's fist is a leash leading down to my neck. It's made of slick black leather similar to his belt, only this one is thinner. While he still makes a show out of his ownership to the crowd, I eye my master.

I'm back in the heady feeling that is subspace and I am lost, so lost in it. By connecting the leash to our sacred collar, Hudson stirred something dormant in me, forcing me into complete surrender, stronger and more potent than simply being called his pet.

My hormones seize control over my consciousness, taking the wheel. I'm of no use to myself, no use at all to anyone or anything except being Hudson's pet.

Hunger mounts at my center, my breasts gravitating to the ground. The smoke tickles the tips of my already hypersensitized nipples, adding to the arousal of the looming, powerful figure of my owner.

His suit jacket stretches against his hard, sinewy muscles, his cock proudly erect in his pants. His chin strong, and jaw locked firmly in place. He's a handsome angel, a God-made sculpture, my other half.

"Come on, Avery." His eyes find mine after he's finished establishing his dominance and possession of me to the rest. "Let's take a walk."

Under his care, I do it easily. I crawl on my hands and knees behind Hudson who takes me around the perimeter free of people.

His gait is slow, exuding assertiveness without being obnoxious about it. He's calm and peaceful, the alpha male who doesn't need to declare his position in the pack. He just is, and when they see him through glowing eyes and hard dicks and sopping pussies, they know that.

I lift my head high as Hudson parades me to them. I'm no longer afraid of the man who narrows his eyes at me while fucking another man's ass. I don't dread the woman giving me sinister looks while another woman holds her from behind and fingers her cunt.

The young woman masturbating on her knees all by herself while moaning and leveling her eyes with me doesn't scare me, either.

No one, not a single one of them, will cross this invisible line when Hudson takes ownership of me the way he does.

I embrace their reactions to the show we're putting on. More than embrace, I accept them. I get fucking wet and turned on by them. My fear fades, and in its place appears a new sentiment, one I haven't fully felt these past four months of my whirlwind engagement to Hudson.

It's what he told me about in the car, what I couldn't wrap my mind around until this very moment. The feeling of *belonging*, of not being judged for our unique relationship and its intricacies, it's a vivid concept, alive and present.

It can happen for us.

We just have to figure out how.

During our walk, my hand lands on a small, plastic artifact. The vibrator. Excited about my ability to please him, I stop my movements, curl my fingers around it and swing it up like a trophy.

Hudson doesn't stop, though. He continues pacing forward and I stay still, hoping he'd notice I'm no longer moving. He doesn't, which I assume he does on purpose, resulting in the leash yanking on my collar.

He stares at me behind his shoulder. "You'll have to do that one on your own, blue. My pet does not cut corners."

My lips part and I'm pretty sure my disappointment of not thinking about it first registers on my face.

Scratch that, I'm sure he sees it. Hudson spins fully, stalking toward me. Without a hint of emotion seeping out of his eyes, he angles himself lower and says, "You did well to point it out. I still need you to do it on your own."

Relief washes over me, and I smile. I'm so into my character that when Hudson caresses my cheek, I twist my face to his hand, lapping my tongue at the inside of his palm.

Warmth flashes behind his eyes, masked by darkness in an instant. "Good girl. Such a good little girl."

He straightens, bringing his wet palm to his nose. Hudson inhales it, then continues walking without wiping it off. I almost come from the gesture, until he tugs me to start walking again.

With every sway of my hips, my clit rubs between my thighs, my skirt chafing my sensitive backside. Fluid runs down my legs, and the view of Hudson as my owner makes it damn near impossible for me not to spontaneously combust.

I can't say it, and succumbing to it, defying him, is in no way an option. Thankfully, on this round when we return to where we started, Hudson's stride comes to a halt. He watches me, crouching to my eye level as I make it to him.

"Now, little." He unhooks the leash from the ring of my collar, then wedges a sanitizing wipe in the barely there space separating my collar and neck. "Go get it for your master."

I'm eager to do it, pivoting to accomplish the task I failed in the past.

Before I can advance toward it, Hudson's Master voice calls out to me, "Oh, and pet?"

I swivel my head back.

His arms are crossed over his chest, his lips form a straight, strenuous line.

A whole eternity transpires between us.

And then it's there. "Use your mouth."

CHAPTER ELEVEN
Hudson

A sense of adoration commands every particle of my body. My gaze hones in on my fiancée's ass as she advances toward the vibrator. *Our* vibrator.

The farther she gets from me—which isn't a lot—the more the smoke curls around her. It licks at her body, envelopes her, then simmers away. Her prowl is determined without being rushed, brimming with intent, and needs to satisfy me without compromising the fun of our game.

She's magnificent. Perfect.

She makes me so goddamn proud.

I divide my attention between her and the rest, keeping an eye on them like I promised her I would. You'd think those who came, who reached their climax, would disperse.

They don't.

I see the faces, recognize the bodies, noticing they haven't left. They haven't even made room for the few others who keep trickling in.

They might've done it any other day, with any other woman. Not my Avery.

Eventually, she stops, the muscles on her shoulders moving as she lifts one hand to hold the vibrator. It's not visible from where I'm standing. It doesn't have to be. I can tell it is.

The raised hand appears next to her neck, the pink pocket rocket standing out in the dark. Dutifully, she pulls out the sanitizing wipe out of her collar and lowers it to her elbows to wipe it clean.

What I wouldn't pay to be at her front, study her face closely as she's inches above the floor. She's obeying orders I commanded her in silence, being my good little girl. I'd never again hesitate to step up and be her Master.

My eyes are locked on her, mesmerized by her, while I arrange the area for when she returns. I bend to grab one of the long, black silk cushions that I kicked out of the way, tossing it on the floor and adding another one parallel to it. Once done, I swing the chair I sat on behind them, sitting on it with my legs sprawled in front of me.

She returns to all fours when I'm done fixing our setting, turning to me.

"Crawl to me." My voice rumbles over the music, above the grunts and screams and dirty talk surrounding us. "Be my good little pet and crawl to me, Avery."

A hint of a dark smile plays on her lips. Shadows are cast on her beautiful features to hide it, but there's also darkness seeping out from her insides. Neither she nor I have done anything remotely close to this in the past, sinister to the core and yet so fitting for us.

She heeds my instructions. Right hand is up, hitting the floor, and the left one follows. Her knees drag on the floor, her body moving seamlessly according to the music.

This immaculate seducer has an immaculate ear to match. I can't wait to be inside of her.

"You did so well," I say those simple words when she's at my feet. Simple, yet holding a hefty meaning in them, for this moment, for past moments. For every other moment we'll ever have together.

The corners of her eyes crinkle and I can tell she gets it.

Before relieving her of the vibrator, I drag my thumb below her bottom lip down to her chin. I trail the slobbery path, my breaths slowing as I *feel* as well as watch the erotic sight of her spit.

"Such a good girl. *My* good little girl." I open my palm facing up beneath her chin, indicating for her to drop the vibrator into my hold.

It lands in my hand, the saliva covering it sticking to my skin. The addition to the dry spit from before is another shot of arousal to my core. They're both a sign of her complete submission, a token of her admiration.

Of giving up a part of herself to a man who would never betray her love and trust.

The same part of me she holds captive, which I'll never want to reclaim.

I take out another wipe out of my back pocket, cleaning the vibrator one last time. The adrenaline, my painfully hard dick, and my immense need to fuck her will never crowd my sense of responsibility to her.

"Take my shoes off," I command her. Technically, it's out of character, not in line with the rules.

And so fucking what?

Fuck people. Fuck them and their set of rules.

Their rules won't make Avery hold on to her breath, won't harden her nipples into tight, pointy nubs.

Others' rules won't.

Ours will.

The shock of lust washes over Avery, taking residence in her. In a graceful movement, Avery bows to my feet. The locks of brown hair hide her work on my shoelaces, although it doesn't matter. Because I feel it.

Once the shoelaces are untied, she takes off one shoe, then the other, and places them neatly to the side.

"I'm so pleased with you." I comb my fingers through her hair and stand up.

Her wide eyes follow me, her clear blue darkening, the taller I rise. She's glued to my hands as I open the button of my pants, roll down the zipper and pull my cock out. It stands erect, swollen with its wet tip in her face.

"Use your teeth to pull them down, all the way to my ankles."

My nostrils flare, having Avery stretch up beneath me. She makes herself tall on her fingertips, her chest opening in the process and giving me a view of the words I wrote on her.

The claim.

PROPERTY OF HUDSON KENT.

She sure as fuck is.

Avery lengthens to her maximum height, and her teeth still don't reach my waistband. She bites the side of her lips, and a second later her face lights up.

It always does when she figures out a new way to please me.

She bares her teeth, sinking them cautiously into the fabric of my pants. Her ass, that round fucking ass I'm dying to pound into, it sways as she moves back and she pulls my pants to the floor.

"Very clever, little." I stroke her hair, and she wiggles her butt in joy before returning to her assignment.

This round of stripping me isn't like the first one. Nothing is separating her teeth, lips, and chin from my thigh as she angles her head and bites the leg band of my boxer briefs.

Her hot, wet chin grazes my thigh, her full lips lighting up my nerve endings like fireworks on the goddamn Fourth of July. My cock jerks, my balls tightening.

I want to have my come mark her face.

And I will. Another day.

Mimicking her earlier ministrations, Avery has my boxers down around my ankles. She looks up at me behind her thick lashes, obedient in her anticipation for further instructions.

"Face the room." I motion with my chin to the crowd. "Sit up on your knees, right there on the cushions, closer to them."

She obeys, and I kick off my pants and boxers to position myself behind her. My cock presses the crack of her ass, my fingers wrap around the front of her neck just in time to catch her gasp.

"See those people?" I yank her dress to her knees, unsnapping her bra.

She hums, and her skin breaks in goosebumps beneath my hand.

"It's not about them." With an arm wrapped to her front, I angle Avery's body forward while stroking her clit. "It's about you. About you feeling comfortable in our skin, even in public. It's about you letting go of work, about you remembering that no matter who's around you, there's only one person in this entire universe you should think about pleasing. Moan if you acknowledge it."

She does, though there's hardly any strength to the sound. Her whole body is weak, relying on me to hold her up. And I don't plan to disappoint her.

"They see it too." I slip the vibrator to the hand that rubbed her, still not turning it on.

"They see the writing,"—my left hand presses my cock to her dripping entrance—"they see how I hold you,"—I tilt her lower, tap my cock to her clit, and put my mouth to her ear—"and now little, they're going to see me fuck you."

I hold her in place, pull my hips back, then slam into her cunt. Her scream pierces the room, her head dropping as if someone punched her chest. Avery's walls clench around me, sucking me into her.

"That's it, baby." My thrusts are slow, but ruthless. The others around us fade into a blur, and there's only me and her. "Let me hear that voice. Show me how you love having my cock deep inside you."

Another moan runs up her chest and out of her mouth. There's an edge, a rawness to it, and she lets it rip whenever I pound into her, over and over and over again. My teeth graze the flesh of her shoulder, taking a bite and sucking her sweet skin.

We're a mess of limbs and grunts and moans. In the midst of the chaos, my thumb flicks on the vibrator that's already on her clit. On an impulse, she grabs my forearms, holding on for dear life.

"You know I've got you," I murmur, keeping the vibrator just above her clit, gliding it up and down.

The tender touch drives her crazier than what would happen if I straight-up pressed it to her. Her fingernails scratch my skin hard. I would've bled had I not been wearing my shirt, although I can't imagine I would've cared either way.

I'm deep into pulling out and shoving myself back inside her, into teasing her with the vibrator. I press it a little harder, move it to her thigh, then circle the hood of her pussy. While I feel her pulse in my heart, I tap the vibrator on her like I did with my cock, the vibrations racing through me as well.

I can see her tits bounce, I can feel her sweat dampening my shirt and vest, and my ears are deaf to anything but her cries of pleasure.

It's high fucking time I give us both what we want.

"You ready to come?"

Her answer is a clipped moan like she can't get it out fast enough with how much she wants it. My balls tighten, my muscles tense, and I fix the vibrator to her cunt with every ounce of power I have left in me.

"Come, Avery. Be my good little girl and come on my cock."

She gasps in a high-pitched tone, sucking in her stomach, and then she comes. Short, tortured cries fill my ears, and it's so hot—*she's* so hot—that in one push, I empty myself deep inside her.

As my cum shoots out of my cock, she knows the scene is over, allowing herself to speak. My name is a plea, a petition, a song of love on her lips. I pull out of her one last time, fixing her dress up her body before I do anything else.

"You're my entire heart, little." I lower her to her back to rest there until I get dressed, kissing her eyes, mouth, and ears. "My entire fucking heart."

CHAPTER TWELVE
Avery

Our home is clean, fresh, and welcoming. Ours.

Hudson carries me in his arms to our bedroom, walking past the bed and straight into the ensuite. Without a word, he switches on the vanity lights that cast a warm glow to the bathroom, then places my feet on the floor gently like I'm made of glass.

In the state I'm in, after the night we had at the club, it might as well be the truth.

"Hands up, my love."

He's taking off the dress we were given at the club, unfastening the clasp of my bra. My dress, shoes, and ripped thong were left behind. Hudson hadn't retrieved his suit as well, hadn't changed in his rush to get us out of there. He didn't want to delay the aftercare phase longer than necessary.

When he offered them payment for the clothes, Chrissy declined, murmuring something about the show covering our costs. I didn't really hear their conversation, my consciousness was not quite back to earth at that point. I had no reason to, either.

I have Hudson to look after me, and that's everything this girl would ever want.

"Stay here," he tells me in a tender yet authoritative voice.

Once I nod, he drags the bathroom bench to where I'm standing, pressing my shoulder in a gentle command to help me sit down.

"I'm running us a warm bath. Be right back."

My head, heavy with the ups and downs and the weight of today, barely tilts toward him. Despite the lethargy taking over me, I want to look at my fiancé so badly that I find it in me to do it.

Through hooded eyes and a ghost of a smile, I whisper to him, "Thank you."

He kisses my forehead, stalking off to start the water and shuck off his clothes.

I'm left staring at the narrow floor-to-ceiling mirror, and I can't help but love what I see. Not my glazed eyes, messy sex hair, or ruddy cheeks. Not the scraped knees, although it does give me the thrill to remember how I crawled for my Master.

It's Hudson's writing. I run my fingertips over the letters, seeing them for the first time. They complement my collar, an expression of my eternal devotion to him.

"Hudson?" I find my voice, barely.

"Yes?" I don't blink before he crouches at my feet. "Everything okay?"

"Everything's perfect."

Our fingers link together, and for the longest moment all I see is him, and I'm his everything.

"Tea?"

"Later."

"Little." His stern expression cracks, and he does his best to suppress his smile. "What did we say about communication?"

I return his smile, untangle my hands from his, and lower myself from the chair and unto the floor. His legs stretch out, arms ready to accept me into a hug. It's a choreographed dance, one we've practiced many times.

My cheek rests on his broad chest, my hands circling his neck, my mouth saying what I wouldn't tell anyone else but him. "Is it crazy that I want to keep what you wrote about me on my body? Just for another day?"

"It would be my honor." Hudson, in a possessive, loving gesture grips my chin, dragging my lips to brush against his. "I'll make sure not to scrub the area."

"Thank you." I kiss his cheek before he carries me to the steaming bath. "Sir."

EPILOGUE
Avery

Hudson puts down his fork and knife, his plate clear of the eggs and bacon I fixed for us. "I have a proposition for you."

We sit in the breakfast room next to each other at the round table the day after Halloween. The paned window overlooks our garden where, among other flowers, I planted two beds of blue carnations. They're identical to the first bouquet he sent me, another constant reminder of his love.

I lower my coffee mug to the table, curious as to what he has to say, what more could he offer after giving me his heart, a promise of marriage, and a collar?

"I'm listening."

"It's not a demand, remember. It's only a proposition." He sits up straight, shoving his plate to the side.

He clasps his hands, interlaces his fingers, and sets his forearms on the table.

CFO Hudson is here.

Reverting to the coworker he respected, I place my hands in my lap and nod. "A proposition, okay."

"I don't want last night to be a fluke." His brow furrows, and while his tone isn't Sir's, it doesn't lack a smidge of authority. "I don't want us to have a moment here, a second there. I want to have countless shared hours, I want you to have time to hang out with Jen, to go out on double dates with her and Briar."

He cups my cheeks, pulling me to him into a deep, passionate kiss. It's full of promise and sincerity, showing me his intention through his lips as well as through his voice. His forehead presses against mine, and I refuse to believe anyone is more handsome than he is right now. Just the way he is in his white T-shirt and jeans, his messy hair, and his unshaven cheeks.

When he's mine.

I don't interrupt him, don't reiterate the importance of my job. He knows how strongly I feel about it. He's not going to ask me to quit, I can sense it. So I keep listening.

"I want us to have a family."

I cover his palms in mine, blinking to cast away the rise of upcoming tears. "I do too."

"Then what do you think about us starting our own company together?"

Thoughts race through my mind a mile a minute. Some of them are laced with doubt, most are hell fucking yes. "Are you serious?"

"Dead serious." He pulls back from me without releasing my hands. His eyes crash harder into mine when draws our palms to his chest, to the steady beat of his heart.

He means it. He actually means it.

"We both worked long enough to know the retail industry inside-out, we have the drive, the best working relationship anyone could ask for." His palm squeezes on mine, his chest puffing as he continues his pitch, "We can have the company, have more time together, be there for our future children's soccer practices or guitar lessons or whatever they choose. We can make it work, blue. I'm sure we can."

While he speaks, the future becomes a reality. I can see it all, and God, do I want it.

My smile tears at the corner of my lips. "Yes, Hudson, the answer is yes."

"Really?" His sudden change from self-assured to stunned is almost comical, except I can't laugh, not right now.

I'm too fucking excited to do anything other than…be excited I guess.

"Yes, really!" I hop out of my seat, making a smooth landing in his lap. "Can we start today?"

His large hand tucks a loose strand behind my ear, his touch sending warm, fuzzy chills down my spine.

"You have just made me the happiest man."

I bathe in his praise, hotter than the crackling fire in the living room, more comforting than a late morning in bed. It engulfs me the same as his arms do, caresses me the same as his kisses on my cheek. It's everything I could ever dream of.

And here it is, my reality.

"I love you, little," he whispers in his husky, bedroom voice.

My head drops to the crook of his neck, and I breathe in his skin.

"I love you too. Forever."

About the Author

Writing edgy spicy novellas, addicted to HEAs, and an avid plant lady.

Stay in Touch!

Newsletter for new releases: https://bit.ly/3c3K2nt

Instagram: https://bit.ly/3QQ3Nh4

TikTok: https://www.tiktok.com/@evamarkswrites

Facebook Group: https://bit.ly/3LnFpln

Website: https://www.evamarkswrites.com/

My books: https://amzn.to/3pnp5XE

Have you read book 1 in the Blue series?

Little Blue

I worked for Hudson Kent for years.

He's not a man you refuse.

But I did.

Because no matter how much I wanted him, chasing the sexy, older CFO would've ruined the reputation I worked so hard to build. It just wasn't a risk I was willing to take.

Until now.

Hudson isn't my boss anymore. There's nothing stopping us from acting on our mutual attraction and acting out every dirty fantasy we've ever had.

So, if he calls me now, there's only one reply I can give.

Yes, Sir.

TW: Bondage, BDSM, edging a bit of degradation and a whole lot of love.

Available on Amazon.

Coming December 2022

Toy Shop

Time to strap on, because class is about to start…

Working in an adult toy shop doesn't make me an expert on the matter. Quite the opposite, actually. My experience with my last boyfriend all but destroyed my interest in it.

Until billionaire Alistair Cromwell bulldozed his way into my life.

He's unlike anyone I've ever known—dominant, harsh, but oddly tender. And he's more than willing to educate me on every product in the shop.

In fact, he insists on it.

He tells me I'm his good girl. That only I can save him from his demons. I want that desperately. But I also want the one thing he doesn't think he can ever give me.

His heart.

Well, he's about to learn that while I'm not worldly when it comes to sex, I do know a thing or two about love.

And I'm going to teach him every bit as much as he's taught me…

TW: Bondage, BDSM, edge play, breath play, sex toys, a bit of degradation, death of a relative, past trauma.

Available for pre-order.

Made in the USA
Columbia, SC
28 October 2022